# DUNG BEETLES

by Martha E. H. Rustad

PEBBLE
a capstone imprint

Pebble Explore is published by Pebble, an imprint of Capstone.
1710 Roe Crest Drive
North Mankato, Minnesota 56003
www.capstonepub.com

**Library of Congress Cataloging-in-Publication data is available on the Library of Congress website.**
ISBN 978-1-9771-2315-2 (library binding)
ISBN 978-1-9771-2649-8 (paperback)
ISBN 978-1-9771-2323-7 (eBook PDF)

Summary: Text describes dung beetles, including where they live, their bodies, what they do, and dangers to dung beetles.

**Image Credits**
Capstone Press, 8; Shutterstock: Alta Oosthuizen, 23, Anna Seropiani, 1, CP7 Photography, 7, DaneMaxwell, 11, evenfh, 18, hakuna_jina, 10, Heiti Paves, 9, Henk Bogaard, Cover, Henrik Larsson, 24, IanRedding, 13, Janny2, 20, Jay S Barton, 27, Johan Swanepoel, 14, Petrik Jakab, 6, PRILL, 19, Sakdinon Kadchiangsaen, 25, Sunet Suesakunkhrit, 17, Villiers Steyn, 5

**Editorial Credits**
Editor: Hank Musolf; Designer: Dina Her; Media Researcher: Morgan Walters; Production Specialist: Tori Abraham

Printed in the United States of America.
PA117

# Table of Contents

Words in **bold** are in the glossary.

# Amazing Dung Beetles

Yuck! That smell can mean only one thing. Poop!

Many animals want to get away from that bad smell. But not dung beetles.

The stink catches their attention. They fly toward the smell as fast as they can. Dung beetles want to get to the poop before it dries out!

Dung is another word for animal
poop. Dung beetles eat dung.

Dung beetles are a kind of **insect** called a beetle. Beetles have a hard covering over their soft wings. There are thousands of kinds of dung beetles. They are sometimes called tumble bugs.

# Where Dung Beetles Live

Where's the poop? Dung beetles live wherever animals poop. So they live nearly everywhere in the world. They do not live in very cold places, such as Antarctica.

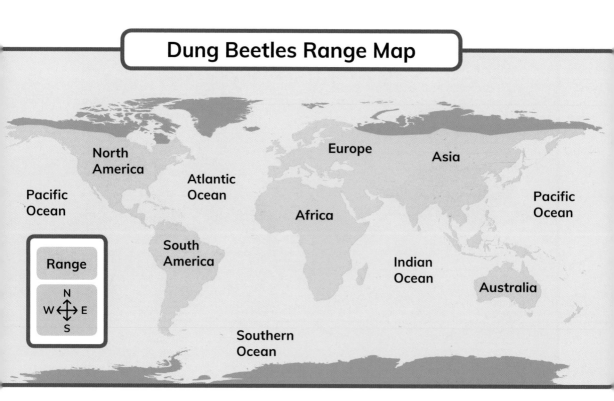

## Dung Beetles Range Map

North America

Europe

Asia

Pacific Ocean

Atlantic Ocean

Pacific Ocean

Africa

Range

South America

Indian Ocean

N
W E
S

Australia

Southern Ocean

Dung beetles have different **habitats**. Some live in deserts. Others live in forests or grasslands.

Some dung beetles follow the animals whose dung they like to eat. Some use the sun and stars as they move. This helps them know how to get from piles of dung back to their homes.

roller dung beetle

Scientists put dung beetles into three groups. These groups are based on how they use poop.

Rollers make dung into balls. They roll them away. Then they bury the balls. Sometimes they eat them. Other times they lay eggs in them.

Tunnellers dig holes under dung. These beetles make underground homes. They live close to where they find their food.

Dwellers bury themselves in poop. These beetles live inside the dung pile. They lay eggs there.

dweller dung beetles

# Dung Beetle Bodies

A dung beetle is an insect. Its rounded body has three parts. Its mouth parts and **antennae** are on its head. Antennae help it find dung.

The middle section is its **thorax**. Its legs and wings are attached here. It has six legs and two wings. A hard cover protects its two soft wings.

The back end is called its **abdomen**. This section holds its stomach and other organs.

wing cover

thorax

wing

abdomen

Some dung beetles have flat heads that are shaped like scoops. Some have legs that are shaped like paddles. These parts help them form dung into round balls.

Dung beetles have strong legs. They dig into dung, and they dig underground.

Rollers move dung balls along the ground. Some of these dung balls are as big as tennis balls! The beetles move upside down and backward as they roll.

Some dung beetles have horns. These pointed parts stick out from their heads.

Dung beetles use their horns to fight. Sometimes they fight over the freshest piles of poo. Sometimes they fight over mates. They fight over dung balls. Dung beetles will steal dung balls from other beetles.

Most dung beetles are brown. But some can be green or red. Some of the colors look shiny.

# Eating and Drinking

Dung beetles eat poop. But not all animal dung is the same. Animal dung has parts of the meal the animal ate.

Some dung beetles eat poop only from herbivores. These animals eat only plants. Others eat dung only from meat-eaters, or carnivores. Many dung beetles eat all kinds of dung.

Adult dung beetles do not drink water. They get water from their food.

Animal dung has both solid and liquid parts. Adult dung beetles suck up the liquid parts of poop. Young dung beetles eat the solid parts of poop.

Some dung beetles eat only poop. Others also eat rotting mushrooms, leaves, or fruit.

# What Dung Beetles Do

Splat! A big, stinky pile of animal poop hits the ground. Dung beetles from all around will flock to it. Sometimes thousands of dung beetles work on a pile of poop together.

A pair of male and female beetles might work together. They roll up a ball of dung. They mate. Later, the female lays eggs inside. After the eggs hatch, some dung beetles take care of their young. Both male and female dung beetles take care of their young.

larva

The bodies of dung beetles change shape as they grow. First, a female lays an egg. Some dung beetles lay several eggs at a time.

Next, a **larva** hatches from the egg. A larva looks like a worm.

The next life stage is called **pupa**. After that stage, the beetle changes into an adult. The adult then leaves to look for more dung. Dung beetles live about three years.

# Dangers to Dung Beetles

Many animals eat dung beetles. Birds follow the balls rolling on the ground. They eat the insects.

Raccoons, foxes, bats, and skunks also eat dung beetles. Some animals eat young dung beetles.

Humans can hurt dung beetles. Farmers sometimes use chemicals on plants. Animals eat the plants. Then dung beetles eat their poop. The chemicals can still be in the poop.

Dung beetles bury poop in soil. This puts **nutrients** back in the soil. They help keep soil healthy and ready for new plants. Farmers can then grow more plants for food.

Dung beetles also move seeds that are inside poop. They put the seeds underground. Then new plants can grow.

Dung beetles help the earth. They make soil better all over the world. And they do it by working with something no one else wants to touch!

# Fast Facts

**Name:** dung beetle

**Habitat:** grassland, forest, desert

**Where in the World:** all continents except Antarctica

**Food:** animal dung, or poop

**Predators:** birds, raccoons, foxes, bats, skunks

**Life span:** about three years

# Glossary

**abdomen** (AB-duh-muhn)—the last body section of an insect

**antenna** (AN-ten-uh)—a body part that sticks up from the head of an insect

**habitat** (HAB-uh-tat)—a place where an animal lives

**insect** (IN-sekt)—a small animal with a hard outer shell, six legs, three body sections, and two antennae; most insects have wings

**nutrient** (NOO-tree-uhnt)—a part of food, like a vitamin, that is used for growth

**larva** (LAR-vuh)—the second stage of an insect's life cycle

**pupa** (PYOO-puh)—the third stage of an insect's life cycle

**thorax** (THOR-aks)—the second body section of an insect

# Read More

Braun, Eric. *Dung Beetle vs. Elephant*. Mankato, MN: Black Rabbit Books, 2018.

Davey, Owen. *Bonkers about Beetles*. New York: Flying Eye Books, 2018.

Marciniak, Kristin. *Astonishing Animals*. Mankato, MN: 12 Story Library, 2018.

# Internet Sites

*Dung Beetle Derby*
kids.nationalgeographic.com/games/action-and-adventure/dung-beetle-derby/

*Dung Beetle: Mighty Recyclers*
kids.sandiegozoo.org/animals/dung-beetle

*Flight of the Dung Beetle*
safeYouTube.net/w/8Fas

# Index